MW01224450

Waking
ALIVE

Alan V. Nelson

To Cheryl,
This is my first to
Canada! It's an honor!
Thank you!
Alan N

Waking Alive
© 2013 by Alan Van Nelson
ISBN-13: 978-1491012574
ISBN-10: 1491012579

Cover image & design by Alan Van Nelson
Author portrait by Van Nelson

alanvnelson.blogspot.com

Printed in the United States of America

ALL RIGHTS RESERVED
No part of this publication may be reproduced, stored in a retrieval
system, or transmitted, in any form or by any means – electronic,
mechanical, photocopying, recording, or otherwise – without prior
written permission.

For Papa

Introduction

The 'Zombie Epidemic' has never been a question of capitalism or exploitation or political leanings, but a moral issue over life and death and what that means to the individual effecting a mass population. While the subject is pure fiction, the undertones are pure reality and the outcome of such can be just as fatal as that first and last bite.

The main questions brought up in George Romero's originals and Robert Kirkman's modern classics are, at their core, really about life and death and the singular, ultimate purpose of the human being. Those are the issues that are going to be brought to the forefront in the next few pages. These questions and their answers are as urgent in those fictional times as they are in our present.

As I researched these particular types of people, I realized that a Preacher, an Artist and a Zombie have one thing in common: their inherent need to spread and feed. The differences lie in what they spread, how they feed and how that affects others in the world. A Preacher wants to spread the love of God and feed the hope of a peaceful eternity; the Artist wants to spread the love of expression and feed the hope of an open mind and free body. The Zombie wants to spread an infection, open your body and feed on your mind.

All three of these purposes, goals and endeavors can infect; some are direly negative and others engagingly positive. They are all utterly simple and just as affecting.

The thing is that we are all human and where our hearts lie determines whether we are walking dead or waking alive.

Waking Alive

It's been days, he thought. *Why haven't I seen another one? Something must've pulled their attention.* The Artist sits back in a wooden chair he found in the building he now sits atop of, alone. He props his feet on the edge and pushes till he's relaxed, reclining and teetering on two legs. Whistling a tune, he taps his fingers on the taped handle of a cricket bat now covered in dried blood.

Just as quickly, he stops whistling and realizes that if he draws their attention, there's no way out but down. *In this world, only the undead could survive that fall.* He sighs quietly. *Stop whistling. Never whistle again.* He lowers the chair down softly to the floor of the roof. Putting his hands on the edge, he eases over to see if there's any on the streets.

The Artist learned a long time ago that minutes mean maybe ten of them; *hours mean thousands.* He has to maintain constant watch, if only to stay sane. While being alone isn't ideal, being dead he likes even less.

After watching for a couple minutes, he reclines back in his chair and looks over what was once New Orleans. The sun is setting but the warm colors bring no warmth; just a promise that tomorrow will be hotter, more rotten and more rank than the last. *I thought this city smelled bad before they took over.* He smiles at his humor. *Still got it.*

His ears twitch at a faint buzzing. "Some idiot fighting them off with something loud," he says. "Pfft. Amateur." He shakes his head and realizes the buzz is gone. His shoulders tense waiting to hear the scream.

A few minutes pass and nothing. He turns his head toward where he thought the buzzing stopped. Still nothing. He shrugs his shoulders and stares back at the sunset.

As the sun dips right above the horizon, the Artist's eyes hang heavy. Beginning to take advantage of the rare relaxation, a loud noise startles him off his chair. Dazed on the floor of the roof, he listens intently and tries to make out what the sound is. It's constant. It's sputtering. It's loud. *It's... buzzing!*

He jumps up and looks over the edge. *Nothing. Where is it? What is it? What is... a chainsaw!* He sees a dark figure racing down the street below. A dark hat covers the face and a duster flows behind them, with a chainsaw smoking by their side. The Artist grabs his bat, runs for the stairwell and makes for the ground floor. Running four floors down, he exits the stairwell and slides across the tile to the front window, getting a closer look.

The man strides down the street in a cloud of exhaust, smoke and fumes. Ready to decapitate anything chomping for brain, the man is tall and stocky with a scarred jaw and enough grizzly facial hair to rub a Great Redwood down to a toothpick. Out of his right eye, he notices the Artist in the window and skids to a halt.

The Artist freezes and stares into the other man's eyes. The chainsaw sputters and idles as the man switches it off, never moving his gaze from the long haired skinny fellow on the other side of the glass. Standing in the street, he sucks his teeth and makes a clicking sound. The Artist doesn't hear it.

"Can you let me in?" asks the man.

The Artist hesitates, unsure of what was said underneath the beard.

The man repeats, "*Can you let me in?*" He opened his mouth wider making sure to enunciate this time.

"I don't read lips," says the Artist.

The man in the street flares his nostrils, parting the hair on his upper lip. He lifts the chainsaw and holds it behind his shoulder, walking toward the front door a few meters away.

Suddenly, the Artist realizes what he's doing and runs to make sure the door is locked. He latches the lock just in time to hear the man try and turn the handle.

"Who are you?" yells the Artist, with his back against the door. "What do you want?"

Nothing happens.

"Answer me, man!"

There's a soft knock and he hears the man's voice.

"May I come in?"

"No. Who are you?"

"I'm surviving. Not for much longer if you don't open the door though. Our friends are making their way up the street."

"You've got a chainsaw, buddy. Use it."

"See, that's the thing. I'm running on fumes."

"I don't have gas here. Move along."

A familiar moan catches the surviving man's ear and a sense of urgency enters his voice.

"Please. Whoever you are. Open the door. They're coming."

The Artist goes back to the window and sees a small group. *I waited too long; wasted too much time on this idiot.* "Gah!" the Artist shouts. "Stand away from the door!"

The man outside slowly backs away. He turns his head slightly to watch the door and the dead with his peripherals.

"I'm coming out, Cowboy. Don't try anything."

The Artist opens the door, bat raised at the ready.

"You're holding the bat wrong," the man says. "You hold..."

"Really?! You think I have a cricket bat to play *cricket*?"

"No. Just making note. Why a cricket bat?"

"Saw it in a movie... nevermind! We don't have time for this."

"Sorry. Can I come in?"

The dead saunter closer.

"No. Who are you?"

The man in black winces. "I'm nobody."

"I need your name. Something."

"I'm... I mean, I was... I *am* a Preacher."

"Not too sure of your calling, eh? And I thought most of you committed suicide being proved wrong and all."

The Preacher raises an eyebrow.

"Not all of us. Who are *you* then?"

"Well, as long as we're on vocations, I'm an Artist. Enough talk though. You're a Preacher? Good. I guess I have to take care of you now that the sun is going down. I have a bunker near here, but it's through *there*." He gestures toward the stumbling crowd.

"You good to make it through them on just your chain?"

"There's no more than five of them. I'd just as soon circumvent."

"Fair enough, Preacher. I got to tell you though," the Artist says as they both hesitate toward the group. "It's a converted one-room Speakeasy with a steel door I modified. You going to have a problem being in a Speakeasy?"

"No problem at all."

The Artist runs toward the few and takes a head off as he passes. The Preacher runs around them but as he reaches the corner of the building, a couple lunge out in front of him. With no hesitation, he swings the chained blade around to take off both their skulls. Pushing through the slowly collapsing bodies, he runs to catch up with the Artist only steps ahead.

They run for a couple blocks and finally down an alley. It's dark and the door is loud. It echoes through humid air and sweaty streets.

"Closing the door usually draws a few of them. It's a clanger. Hold your ears."

The door makes an awful, loud screeching noise from it's hinges.

The large room is black and dank. It smells of blood and Clorox. The Preacher's boots echo as he takes light steps, making sure he doesn't trip over anything. He hears a match strike and turns around. With long hair stuck to the sweat on his face, the Artist lights a cigarette, takes a drag, then lights a nearby lantern. "Got to have priorities, Preacher."

The Preacher surveys the bar as the light grows. The mirror behind the counter is shattered and no glasses or alcohol are to be found.

"When I found this place, half the booze was gone already. I drank the rest of it."

"When did you find it?"

The Artist smiles. "A couple days ago."

Part I

They both take a seat at the nearest table. In the lantern light, they sit for a while not saying anything; the Preacher with his hat on the table staring blankly into the dark and the Artist reclining with his hands cradling his head.

Artist

So where were you?

Preacher

Huh?

Artist

Where were you?

Preacher

Where was I *what*?

Artist

When all this...

The Artist waves towards the door.

Artist

When all *this* happened.

Preacher

On the way home from church one Sunday afternoon.

Artist

Somebody call you?

Preacher

No. We were listening to the radio and singing along when one of those 'This Is Not A Test' things came on.

Artist

The Early Warning System?

Preacher

Yeah. Except not a cloud in the sky. I changed the station thinking it was a glitch; somebody screwed up or something.

Artist

But it wasn't...

Preacher

It was on every station. The computer voice kept saying to go inside immediately. To not come out except in case of emergency. There were no details.

Artist

How did your family react?

Preacher

We didn't know what to do. I just drove home and my wife fixed lunch like normal. We sat down at the table, prayed and started eating.

Artist

You didn't check the TV or internet?

Preacher

Nope. We took breaks from that on Sundays.

Artist

Then how did you find out?

Preacher

My little girl always used to sit so she could look out the window. She had stopped eating and was just staring. I had my back to the window, but my wife looked out and saw what my daughter was looking at. There was a man...

He swallows hard and stares off into nothing.

Artist

It was one of them?

Preacher

My wife tapped me on the arm and said, 'Honey...' and pointed. I wiped my mouth and turned around. I couldn't believe it...

The Artist could see faintly that the Preacher's eyes were welling up.

Artist

Did you freak out?

Preacher

No. We sat with our mouths on the floor. My little girl didn't know what it was. My wife and I were kids of the eighties and nineties though. Pop culture had so ingrained this image in our head that it felt like a dream when it happened. When it *actually* happened.

Artist

I'm right there with you. George Romero was the man. I remember hearing he committed suicide though; he felt like he contributed to all this in a way.

Preacher

I remember that too.

The Preacher wipes his eyes.

Artist

So what did you do about the guy

outside of your house?

Preacher

Nothing. Didn't have to. We heard a loud whistle and looked over and saw our neighbor, Steve, holding a rifle a little ways up the street. The thing turned and bang! Down it went. That's when we reacted. Especially my little girl.

Artist

Screaming?

Preacher

Oh yeah. She finally stopped after a while though. She just sat in the corner. We didn't know how to explain it to her. We didn't ever imagine it would've gotten this bad either...

Artist

...much less actually happen in the first place.

Preacher

Exactly. The movies, the TV shows; we should've been more prepared.

Artist

There's no way we could've known though.

Preacher

I guess. But we all heard the news reports and rumors of militaries and cities having drills for this sort of thing. I thought they were all trying to be relevant to pop culture.

Artist

'Political Hipsters?'

Preacher

Something like that.

Artist

Yeah.

Preacher

What about you? What's your story?

Artist

It's age-old really: a show in Atlanta one day and slaughtering mobs of the undead the next.

Preacher

How did you find out?

Artist

When I remember it, it feels like I just walked into a room and stumbled upon the stumblers. A curator threw a rooftop after-party and there were about fifty or so of us up there; half of us passed out. I think we all

woke up to screams coming from the streets
below. Sirens wailing.

Preacher

Sounds like a movie.

Artist

We thought they were filming
something, yeah. I, for sure, had never heard
screams like that. We all ran for the roofs
edge. Within seconds, some of the people
next to me just threw themselves over.

Preacher

What for?

Artist

They just gave up, I guess. It was my
first inclination too. 'The world's gone to crap,
might as well save myself some pain.' I
remember thinking that. What sucks though...
the fall didn't kill some of them. Some were all
broken and oozing on the sidewalk moaning
till a group of... well, till they had nothing left
to moan with.

Preacher

Wow...

Artist

Weirdest thing I'd seen happened that
day too. We were all on top of the roof,
scared out of our minds; my girl's rocking

back and forth like this...

He wraps his arms around his chest and ducks his head, softly moaning.

Artist

And this couple to my left, right? The guy looks at his girl and says 'Are you ready?' And the girl, all teary, shakes her head yeah.

Preacher

Were they ready for what?

Artist

Apparently ready to dive bomb, hand-in-hand, off the side of the building. Tried to stop them...

He takes a deep, long drag from his cigarette.

Artist

I was just in time to watch them fall over. I watched them fall until their faces smashed into the sidewalk and their bodies crumple like accordions. What makes it weird is that, as far as I could tell, their hands stayed together. That really made me appreciate the time I had left with my girl. Then I threw up for a while.

Preacher

Wow...

Artist

Yeah. You said that. What's the weirdest you've seen?

Preacher

Weirdest?

Artist

Yeah.

Preacher

Probably my wife peeling off one of their faces with a spokeshave.

Artist

What's that?

Preacher

It's used in woodworking. It's like a hand-plane except the handles are on either side of the blade.

Artist

Are you serious? Your wife's crazy! But that didn't kill it. Couldn't have.

Preacher

It didn't. That's the first time I used this chainsaw on something other than a tree.

Artist

I was going to say: the way you carry that thing you'd think it was attached to your arm or something.

Preacher

It's sentimental. Don't want to lose it.

Artist

Why's that?

Preacher

It was a gift from them: my wife and little girl.

Artist

Yeah? And where are they now?

Preacher

Hewn down...

Artist

You took your blade to them? Well what made you want to go and do that? Go crazy with the rest of us?

Preacher

They were bitten and...

Artist

Ah. I figured you wouldn't just start cutting them into lumber. You don't seem like the type. You might look like the type though...

Preacher

Do you have anyone?

Artist

Nope. Not anymore. Everybody I cared about I had to knock around with my bat. Stained with blood from a couple hundred kills. Crazy days. So did they beg you to end it for them or you just did it when they went into a coma?

Preacher

This is a little more personal than the last topic. Kind of heavy for a first meeting, don't you think?

Artist

We just ran away from a mini-horde and made a pretty big racket slamming the door back. I'd say they are outside right now and we'll just have to wait till morning and see how it is then. There's nothing better to do except sit and get to know each other. Besides, I don't like sitting quiet in a dark room. It gives me the creeps.

Preacher

That gives you the creeps?

Artist

Funny huh? With everything outside, me in a quiet, dark room is creepy.

Preacher

You must be afraid of being alone.

Artist

Something like that, but I have to deal with it nowadays. So back to my question: how did you end them?

Preacher

I didn't end them. The infection did.

Artist

Wait. You didn't kill them till *after* the infection took them?

Preacher

Right.

Artist

Are you *serious*?

Preacher

Yes. What's the problem?

Artist

So you let them suffer?

Preacher

If that's how you want to put it. I did what I thought was right.

Artist

I suppose you want me to believe that *God* wanted it that way?

Preacher

Where's *that* coming from?

Artist

You're a Preacher, right?

Preacher

Right. But I'm trying to understand your problem.

Artist

My problem is that you probably want me to believe God wanted it that way. Am I right?

Preacher

A little insensitive, aren't we?

Artist

You should've helped them end it.

Preacher

I just buried the twice-dead corpses of my wife and child and I let them die of *this* because there is no cure. I let them die because it's not my place to take a life with a soul. But, they weren't human when they died the second time. They were organisms. They had unquestioning needs for consumption and destruction. *This...*

The Preacher points violently toward the door.

Preacher

...this is unnatural nature at it's most

severe. Could I blame God? Sure. Did He cause this? No. Did He let it *happen*? Yes. Why? I'll ask him when I see him...

Artist

You let them die in pain and agony and become monsters. Then, as monsters, you kill them?

Preacher

And so you keep pushing?

Artist

I'm not pushing you. I'm trying to understand why only when they become a threat to you, you kill them. When the only life that matters is yours, that's when you end theirs? How *selfish* can you *be!*

Preacher

Please stop.

Artist

No. You should've helped them end it; save them from the pain. *God* would've ended it for them. He's the one you're supposed to model your life after, remember?

Preacher

How do you know what God would or wouldn't do?

Artist

I know He gave up on this place months ago. That's for sure.

Preacher

There are choices only He can make; rights only He has. What right do I, even you, have to kill a human being?

Artist

It's not a right and it's not killing! It's a duty to help your fellow man live and die in peace. It's human responsibility to save them from a living hell, however much longer we're all in it. And right now, with these freaks stumbling around, I'd say we've been there a while.

Preacher

Then why don't you take your own life?

Artist

Excuse me?

Preacher

Yeah. Why don't you just whack yourself around a few times and just end it. You seem to think dying is better than living. And do you see *now* why I didn't want to talk about all this?

Artist

I see.

Preacher

Then why do you persist?

Artist

Because anything is better than the end of the world. Especially like this. Don't you see that's what this is? It's the end, man! All of it: your family, my girl... they're better off just gone.

Preacher

And so again, why don't you just end it? End it all. Take your life if what's after is so much better.

Artist

Isn't Heaven better than this?

Preacher

Yes. But I'm not going to cut my head off to get there. God will take me when it's time. What's your reason?

Artist

I want to see what happens. I'm curious.

Preacher

You're not killing yourself for curiosity's sake? I'm not going to condone suicide, but that's a pretty odd reason.

Artist

Yeah, but aren't you curious who'll win Armageddon? It's either us or them, man. The epic battle between man and monster. It gets me psyched just thinking about it.

Preacher

So it's less curiosity and more an adrenaline rush that's keeping you alive? Blood and gore is what you want the rest of your life to be filled with?

Artist

Under the present circumstances, there's no way around that one. It's all we have. It's great inspiration too. The blues, greens, browns, grays; reds, blacks, purples... all these colors! It's art! Life wasn't nearly as inspiring before. It wasn't as consistently tragic and colorful as it is now... I can only imagine the work I'll create.

Preacher

I'll admit, the first thing I love about fall are the leaves turning because they're dying... but I can't remember the last time I watched someone bleed out and thought, *That's inspiring.*

Artist

That's where your beliefs about death cloud your judgment. People like you are close-minded about everything like that. You see death and think of what's after. You see life and think of eternity.

Preacher

I'm failing to see the downside to my supposed '*close-mindedness.*'

Artist

Well, what about right now; right here? What about this second? That's all that matters. When the future gets here is when we worry about it.

Preacher

What happens if the future happens and it's too late to do anything about it?

Artist

Then you deal with it. You miss too much thinking about the future all the time. There's not much of one to think about anymore anyway.

Preacher

There's always a future. Just maybe not the one we're accustom to thinking about.

Artist

I don't completely disagree with that.

Preacher

And how can you not think about the future... more specifically you're next move, when the world out there is keeping us on our toes twenty-four-seven?

Artist

I don't consider thinking about my next move as the future. I consider that living in the moment. Death, life, sex, blood... what ever is happening in any given moment has priority over all. Time and the future is whatever, man. A moment defines everything. That's the rush. That's the inspiration. That's art!

Bitten

I'm glad I can inspire you...

A cracking voice from behind the bar causes the Artist to fall backward out of his chair and the Preacher to jump to a stiffened stand. A hand reaches up on to the bar followed by a lively groan.

Artist/Preacher

What the...?!

A black man rises from behind the bar and stares at the Artist and Preacher. The lantern light reflects in his glazed eyes.

Preacher

Was he here when we got here?!

Artist

I... I don't know! How long have you

been there?

Bitten

That's not important... Just know that... ooph... I've been bitten... You need to leave...

Artist

There's no where to go. You... you... where's my bat?!

Preacher

Calm down! He's behind the bar. We've got the advantage. And it doesn't look like he's been here for long. He might have been here a few minutes before we ran in. Either way, we don't want to do anything irrational. We're not going to hurt him.

Bitten

Please... it's OK... let him kill me...

Preacher

No. I'm sorry.

Artist

You heard him! It's not for you to decide what I'm going to do and what he wants. Let me do it... Move!

Preacher

No! There'll be no killing here until he's dead. It's not what you want, it's not what he wants. It's just what's right and what I believe.

Agony or not, beliefs are all any of us have right now. And I'm willing to die for mine. *Are you?*

Artist

You are so blinded! It's sad. It's selfish! You would want us to end it for you... or who knows? You're self-righteous enough to preach us all the way to the end aren't you?

Preacher

Will you *stop*? We'll talk about all that in a minute.

The Preacher looks over to Bitten and steps towards the bar.

Preacher

Is there anything I can get you? Anything I can do to make it easier?

Bitten

I'd like a gun... but I'm too weak to pull a trigger...

Preacher

I can understand that. Would you like some water or something? I'm sure we can find you some around here worth drinking.

Artist

Pfft. Not in New Orleans.

The Preacher takes the lantern and a glass from the bar and goes to find the bathroom. The Artist and Bitten stare very tensely at each other.

Artist

I could kill you.

Bitten

OK....

Artist

You going to try and stop me?

Bitten

Nope...

Artist

Nobody is going to miss you right?

Bitten

Just that Preacher, I imagine...

Artist

Preachers always miss things that are too late to help. He's gone in the other room though. Do you really want me to kill you?

Bitten

Yes... Will you do it already?

Artist

I'm weighing my options.

Bitten

It's not as easy a choice... when you ain't afraid of me no more... is it?

The Preacher returns with some water from the sink in the bathroom.

Preacher

Here's some water...

Bitten

Thanks Preacher... but this don't help the bite...

Artist

Nothing does. Nothing will.

Preacher

It's nice to know you're still standing, Old Timer. I fully expected to hear the Artist over here scream like a Banshee and bash your brains in while I was in the toilet.

Bitten

No such luck...

Preacher

Can I help you to a chair at the table? What were you doing back there anyway?

As the Preacher helps Bitten to the table, he explains.

Bitten

I came in to have one last drink... and all the booze was gone... After listenin to y'all talkin... I realized the lanky fella with the itchy swingin arm... had been the reason for all that...

Artist

First come–first serve, Old Man.

They all sit as the Preacher glares at the Artist, not comprehending his lack of sensitivity.

Preacher

So what about you? What's your story?

Artist

I already told you my story.

The Preacher nods toward Bitten.

Preacher

I wasn't talking to you. I was talking to him. What's your story, Friend?

Artist

Yeah, Fleshy... how'd you end up in my bar?

The Preacher rolls his eyes.

Bitten

It's *my* bar actually...

Artist

How's that?

Bitten

The deed's in my name... I own it... It's my place... Says so on the sign outside...

Preacher

I didn't notice the sign.

Artist

Me either. What's it say?

Bitten

My name... As you all aren't too interested in names... I'll let you figure it out when you leave...

Preacher

You can't tell us your name then?

Bitten

Nope...

Artist

Alright then. I have a bone to pick with you now, Preacher.

Preacher

Is this really the time?

Artist

Got any place better to be?

Preacher

Fine. Go ahead.

Artist

I don't get you.

Preacher

We've established this.

Artist

Yeah. But if anyone were to read about this, I'd be considered a villain. Like I have no humanity. You'd look like a stubborn saint. But you don't care about that. You care about something you can't see or hear judging your every move and you forget about the people right here, right now!

Preacher

This may seem unfair, but who still has a blood-tipped cricket bat ready to swing at a dying man in his last hours?

Artist

That's what I mean!

Bitten and the Preacher both look at the Artist questioningly.

Artist

Mmm... you're right. I'm going to chill out and then we'll get back to figuring out what to do about the... dead guy.

Bitten

Yup... Thanks for the sensitivity...

Preacher

I can't honestly say you don't make me uncomfortable sitting there. It's not a good feeling sitting near your potential demise no matter how many times you've done it. I can only imagine what it feels like going through it. What's it like? To be bitten, I mean?

Bitten

Hippy here is bein' insensitive... now you're bein' insensitive... don't make me go through it again... Get back to your conversation... it helped keep my mind off of the pain...

Preacher

You're right. I apologize. Let me know if you need any more water.

The Preacher turns to the Artist. The Artist is sitting, again, leaned back in his chair rocking on two of it's wooden legs.

Preacher

Where were we? Everything is art? Even *this* guy?

Artist

Are you sure he's okay? How close is he to turning?

Preacher

A while off... the wound is fresh. We'll be fine for now.

Artist

Alright, good. OK. To be quite honest, most of what I said is bull crap. I had to keep that type of front so my work seemed more mysterious. I doubt I'll ever create again. My biggest inspiration was my girlfriend. Not that I've had time to work anyways. When I did though, she was always there with encouragement and a great eye. But *everything* being art? Probably not. I mean, pain is the catalyst for great work sometimes but most of the greats concentrated on the beauty they imagined, saw and witnessed in their lives and hearts. There was always life in their work. Life is an art form. But it's useless to be so idealistic and positive now.

Preacher

We can agree to disagree on that last part, but I do agree that all life is an art form. Human life, plant life, animal life, eternal life... all of it. The true Artist had quite the imagination.

Artist

Jesus again? You do realize this 'event' kind of contradicts all that stuff about Him, right?

Preacher

I'd be lying if I said that I hadn't thought about it. I struggle with faith these days. I struggle with hope. I struggle with fear and worry and confidence in Jesus. I struggle thinking that God would let all of this happen. All of this death and loss... it's a weight and it feels like it's breaking my back sometimes.

Artist

So you doubt what you say you believe in?

Preacher

I struggle with the notion that maybe it's not real. Maybe it's not worth it.

Artist

An *honest* Preacher? An honest *Christian*? Wow...

Preacher

I'm sure you don't have to worry about that stuff because you don't even believe in anything.

Artist

I never said what I believed in. I think you just assumed that because of how I define myself. A lot of Artists are stereotyped as people who don't believe in anything. Truth is, most of us just don't like confrontation.

Preacher

A little ironic considering you almost beat a guy to death a couple minutes ago.

Bitten nods his head and grunts in agreement.

Artist

And that's funny coming from a Preacher mowing down the undead with a chainsaw.

Bitten

Touché, Preacher...

The Preacher smiles.

Preacher

I know, right?

A quiet passes over the room as they study their surroundings. Bitten takes a swig of water.

Preacher

I was thinking about something the other day.

Artist

Besides survival?

Preacher

Yeah. I have to sometimes. Don't you?

Artist

I used to like to whistle. It drew too many though. I try to amuse myself to stay present, but this conversation is about as deep as I've been in a while.

Preacher

Deep in thought?

The Artist chuckles.

Artist

That too.

Preacher

Very funny. Don't you want to know what I was thinking about?

Artist

Sure.

Preacher

I was thinking about how this wasn't the first time the dead walked free.

Artist

Lazarus, right?

Preacher

No. But in the same vicinity of time.

Artist

I'm not sure I follow.

Preacher

They weren't like what we've seen out there, I don't think. But the moment Christ died, some of the righteous dead rose and walked around Jerusalem.

Artist

'Righteous dead?'

Preacher

Yeah. Like believers in Jesus that had already died.

Artist

And this is in the Bible?

Preacher

In the book of Matthew actually. Chapter twenty-seven? Yeah. Chapter twenty-seven. Verses... verses fifty-two and fifty-three.

Artist

Hm.

Preacher

What?

Artist

Why just dead believers?

Preacher

I don't know really. I hadn't really thought about that and the Bible doesn't dwell too much on the event.

Artist

But you have a theory?

Preacher

I have a lot of theories.

Artist

I'm sure. What's your theory on these God-walkers then?

Preacher

My theory is this: why would His power not raise people that solemnly rejected Him?

Artist

That's a question. Not a theory.

Preacher

It's part of the deduction. Just answer the question.

Artist

I don't know. Why would he?

Preacher

Why *should* he?

Artist

To give them a second chance?

Preacher

Why would He give them a second

chance when they had a lifetime to decide to follow Him?

Artist

Because He's God and that's what He would do.

Preacher

Would you believe in *that* God?

Artist

No.

Preacher

Why not?

Artist

Because *that* God doesn't have a backbone.

Preacher

You don't believe in a God, but you do believe in something if I understand correctly. But you don't believe in a God that gives too little *or* too much?

Artist

Correct on all counts.

Preacher

What about one that gives just enough and never more than we can handle?

Artist

We've veered from your theory, but I'll humor you. *That* God doesn't exist either. Never will.

Preacher

And why's that?

Artist

Because that's *your* God. I don't believe in *your* God; anyone's God. 'God-walkers' either.

Preacher

Do you regularly *not* believe in something out of spite?

Artist

If I answer and say yes, you'll probably ask if I would've believed in the dead walking around, had I not seen them first.

Preacher

It would've been a natural progression, yes.

Artist

Just tell me your theory about why only dead Christians went and scared the 'Jesus' into people.

Preacher

Witty.

Artist

I try.

Preacher

It's a simple idea, really. I think only dead believers awoke because they were followers without needing His death and resurrection as proof.

Artist

I would've needed proof.

Preacher

And that's OK. To an open heart, Jesus' death and resurrection was an offering of proof.

Artist

I have an open heart.

Preacher

You have an open mind. Two different things.

Artist

I loved. Therefore I have an open heart. And technically speak...

Preacher

Are you really going to argue semantics?

Artist

Point taken. I have to concede that the

Bible talking about ghouls is pretty awesome.
But I used to think the whole concept of these
lovely, little stumblers was awesome too
though.

Preacher

The Bible has a lot of crazy concepts.

Artist

The Bible *is* a crazy concept.

Preacher

Why do you say that?

Artist

You think it's God's word right?

Preacher

Technically...

Artist

Semantics, Preacher?

Preacher

Sorry. Yes. The Bible is God's word.

Artist

Boom. Crazy concept.

Preacher

But *why* is it crazy?

Artist

Because you think that an everlasting,

all-powerful being would take the time to dictate thousands and thousands of words for His glorification?

Preacher

So I'm crazy for *thinking* that or the concept is crazy for *being* that?

Artist

What's crazy is that we're having this conversation in the middle of the end.

Preacher

The end of what?

Artist

Life. At least the way we think of it.

Preacher

You really think that human nature will change though?

Artist

When did I say that?

Preacher

We haven't discussed it, but I assumed you either meant the way we *live* life or the way we *see* life. It was 50/50.

Artist

You're perceptive, Preacher.

Preacher

And hey: I'm sorry for assuming you had no belief system. I'm surprised by a lot these days. You obviously do believe in something. I guess when I'm struggling with my doubt, I am quicker to judge.

Artist

You said a few minutes ago that you'd die for your beliefs. Was that bull crap like my 'everything is art' or...?

Preacher

Absolutely not. Even with doubt, I still know where my faith lies and who has control even in all this chaos. It's when I start to think *I* have control over my life and my death that my doubt comes in. In reality, I'm doubting my capacity to believe and hold on. I'm not doubting His presence and love. That's always there and it never recedes. Romans eight, thirty-eight and thirty-nine, to be specific. The Bible tells me that nothing separates me from His love. When the Bible says it, that's what I have to go on. If I doubt that, then I doubt Him. He'd never forsake me; what else could I do but give my life for Him?

Artist

Like you believe He did for you?

Preacher

Exactly.

Artist

And you look to Him for control over your life and death?

Preacher

I do.

Artist

I don't see control. I've never seen control.

Preacher

Then what do you see?

Artist

I see unrelated events and random chaos breakout, like what's outside. Like what's moaning and groaning and ready to take control over whether you live or die tonight. I don't see God here making sure you don't get bitten. I see your legs running, your hands wielding and your chain spinning as what determines who controls what. Even then, it's not definite. It's whoever is strongest, fittest, fastest and smartest. Always has been, man. It's always going to be that way. 'Survival of the Fittest' I think is what it's called. Whoever has the capacity to survive, survives and thrives. It's random. Like Cancer.

Preacher

So life and death are random, but

whoever is the 'best' is going to be the one who lives? So there's a definite there, right? One has to be a definite 'better' to last longer than the 'not as good?'

Artist

Well, it's not a definite. The 'best' aren't always going to survive. Some chance of cerebral hemorrhage could happen and they just fall over.

Preacher

But, they are the best... why don't they survive even random chance?

Artist

Because you can't be ready for everything. No control, man. It's all random.

Preacher

So chance determines who the 'best' is?

Artist

Yes. Life is a lottery. You pick your numbers and hope they are never called.

Preacher

Do you see the circle you're going in? The contradiction in that type of thinking?

Artist

I'd rather live a contradiction than life

with someone controlling me. At least I can determine contradiction.

Preacher

At the danger of letting this realm of thought drag on way too long, you determining contradiction is control. You don't want control and yet autonomy is the very thing you hold dearest. Where your paint stroke begins and ends, where the photograph is taken and at what angle.

Artist

You can't tell me that your thinking is any more right when you follow a dictatorship.

Preacher

I can tell you that I have choices, just like you do. When I say control, I don't mean enforced and brutal non-negotiations. I mean: God has a plan for me. I can choose to follow it or not. There are rewards for listening and punishment for not.

Artist

So it's a 'do this and you'll be fine or don't and face the consequences?' How is that *not* a dictatorship?

Preacher

If God created life and He knows the best course for it, then who am I to disobey?

Artist

But you do. And using your beliefs here, you sin just like I do. Isn't that punishable by death? God's going to kill you if you don't obey. It's funny that He was King of the Jews and yet He kills someone because they don't listen to Him. It's a *Hitler Complex*. It's a contradiction. You go in circles just like I do.

Preacher

I know it can seem like that, but not one thing I've said has contradicted any other. Yes, I sin. Yes, it's punishable by death. But, with throwing my beliefs in my face, you forget one thing: Jesus, God's Son, already died for me and with that choice of *His*, with *His* blood, *He* gave me a choice. Follow and obey Him or don't. If I do, He'll give me a fantastic eternity full of life and void of chaos. If don't, He'll let me suffer in unending pain. He'll let me die a thousand deaths.

Bitten

Good thing I'll only be dyin' twice then...

Preacher

It's an either/or choice. He's not asking you to do anything He hasn't already done for you. He suffered and He died. God gave His Son to die to give each one of us a choice. It's not control. It's asking you to trust and believe Him. It's not a dictatorship. It's compassion and salvation.

Bitten

At least one of us sees His compassion... I'm gonna take a deep breath... and then just spew out what it is I'm needin' to say... God's compassion is a figment of your imagination, son... If you think that what I'm goin' through is compassion... then you've got a few brains needin' to be eat... Besides that, there's a whole world out there dyin' or dead and dead again... and you're in here givin' us a 'hope and compassion lecture'... Big Ole Jesus is way up in the sky laughin' at us for thinkin' His 'strength and love' were gonna save us... This is Hell, boy... you're in it... you're dead... same as me...

Artist

And who is Jesus to die for us? I didn't ask Him to do it. Of course, I didn't get asked if I wanted my girlfriend to be ripped apart 10 feet away from me either. So I guess there's a lot of people being given choices these days, huh?

Preacher

Yup. Don't forget my wife and child in there with the dead and dead again. I buried them and yet I'm not being realistic for trying to hold onto something? Am I delusional for believing there's a compassionate God that has my life in His hands?

Artist

That's not what I said.

Bitten

Me neither...

Preacher

That's what both of you are implying. You don't have to say it. If you chose to live out the rest of your moments with anger towards someone who never gives us more than we can handle, go for it!

Artist

You're right. That horde out there is not too much to handle on your own. Tell us when you're done. Good luck with that.

Preacher

I'm sorry I have hope. I'm sorry I still have a little faith in humanity! I'm sorry I doubt and I'm sorry I'm still very much alive and still *completely* human. Your choices would be a lot simpler if you only had one thing to do like they do. Walk around dead, feed when you don't even need to and finally die when something stronger and faster caves your skull in. *What do you believe in?!*

Bitten

Miracles...

A few seconds pass and the Preacher and Bitten exchange glances. Even amidst the tension, the two men burst into laughter.

Artist

And we crack jokes? *Really?!*

Preacher

Come on. Even I can appreciate that one. We need a little life around here.

Bitten and the Preacher burst out laughing again.

Artist

You too? There's death surrounding all of this and we're in here joking about stuff when we should be planning how to get out of this.

Preacher

Calm down. We're just busting a gut.

Artist

Shut up.

Preacher

Fine. Fine.

The Preacher and Bitten finally stop

laughing long enough to catch their breath.

Preacher

Listen. What's to plan? When it's light out, then we'll take a peek, see what we're up against and then go from there.

Bitten

I need some water...

Artist

I'll get it this time. Get away from you two for a minute.

The Artist leaves with the lantern, closing the bathroom door behind him; the light flooding through the seems of the doorway, barely lighting Bitten and the Preacher left at the table.

Preacher

So I know you heard our stories. What's yours, Old Timer?

Bitten

Besides being the cliché black fella that gets bit and dies at the end...?

Preacher

Yes. Besides that. Have you waited it out here?

Bitten

Naw... I did somethin' stupid and left... I

was ready to just drink myself to death... then I felt like livin' and went to find some food... I found some... ate it... then on my way back... something tried to eat me... and that's how I come to be bit... When I come back... turns out ole hippy in there drank me out...

Preacher

Sorry about that. I just recently came in to town myself.

Bitten

And where's home...?

Preacher

The Carolinas. North, actually. The Bible belt.

Bitten

I figured something like that... You didn't sound Northern like the other'n... where you reckon he's from...?

Preacher

Not sure. We can ask him when he gets back. But, really: what's your story? How did you find out?

Bitten

It was 'bout mid-afternoon and I seen this fella come in lookin' like he been drunk for days... Then I seen his eyes... Like some gangrene infected 'em... ain't no kind of alcohol do that...

Preacher

What'd you do?

Bitten

I took my sawed-off shotgun from behind the counter... the one regulars think is just for show... and blew his face clean off...

Preacher

All because the gangrene in his eyes?

Bitten

I ain't gonna shoot a man that just looks like some gangrene eat 'em up... I shot 'em in the face 'cause he saw me and started lickin' his upper teeth... he didn't have no lower ones...

Preacher

That's disgusting.

Bitten

Yeah... well try cleanin' all that up and not blowin' chunks before happy hour... It took a while... had to clean him *and* me up... I can still smell it all... To think I used to wish the smell of smoke would wash out of these here walls... kinda miss it now...

Preacher

How long ago was all that?

Bitten

Seems like yesterday... but I'm pretty sure a few weeks... The plague... or whatever the news called it... didn't hit Orleans till a few months after the east coast... We had time to prepare... or not... I chose not to...

Preacher

Why not?

Bitten

With all the people stressin' out and drinkin'... this place had never been so successful... I didn't have time to prepare... I was enjoyin' all the hoopla... I tell ya... REM... the local boys of yours from Carolina... that one *forsaken* song got played a hundred... *two* hundred times a day...

Preacher

Wow. Well, what can I do to make you comfortable?

Bitten

Not talk about it like I'm knockin' on Heaven's door....

Preacher

Dylan.

Bitten

It's a good song...

The Preacher nods in agreement.

Preacher
> Topical.

The two grow silent staring off across the glowing lines of stained wooden tables and chairs. A couple minutes pass.

Bitten
> I lived upstairs.

Preacher
> Really? Right above us? How do you get up there?

Bitten
> There's only an outside entrance... I've sealed off the place though... Nothin' up there I need... And don't be thinkin' there's anythin' you're needin' up there neither... Him too...

Bitten points toward the bathroom.

Preacher
> What's up there?

Bitten
> Any family that could fit in the place... thirty head of zombie at least...

Preacher
> I don't hear any movement. Are they dead?

Bitten

Naw... Old bars like this were built sound proof... Inside and out...

Preacher

I'll tell him later then. We don't need to excite him again.

Bitten

I wish you'd let him kill me, Preacher... but I understand why you won't... I appreciate it even though I don't like it...

The door to the bathroom creaks open and light floods the empty bar.

Artist

You got a cleaner bathroom? Is there an upstairs to this place?

Preacher

There was.

Artist

What happened to it?

Bitten

Closed it up... You drank me outta business... you're not drinkin' me outta home too...

Bitten slyly winks at the Preacher. The Artist roles his eyes, not noticing.

Artist

How's he doing?

Bitten

You can ask me... It's not like I'm contagious...

Preacher

Alright. Alright. Don't antagonize him. How *are* you doing though?

Bitten

I can feel it spreading... I'm a lot weaker...

Artist

How much time do you think you have?

Preacher

He's been talking, but I think he's getting close to passing out. I've just been trying to keep him alert. It's just a waiting game after he goes into a coma though. Is there anything you need from me?

Artist

Nope.

Preacher

Old Timer?

Bitten

Just keep talking... I've enjoyed the tension...

Preacher

I've actually enjoyed the conversation too, now that I've had a couple minutes to cool down and really appreciate our circumstances.

Artist

Ha!

Preacher

Yes. I see the irony. Let's get back to it now that you've had your potty break.

Artist

Fine. I think this is as good a time as any to bring this up anyway. It's on the tip of our tongues, so why not?

Preacher

And what's that?

Artist

What do you think about death?

Preacher

I think it's pretty evident by what we've talked about already. But in what capacity do you mean?

Artist

Like, the *act* of death.

Preacher

I've talked a lot already. Why not tell me what you think and we can discuss that.

Then we'll see how we differ. Seems to be a pretty good formula so far, yeah?

Artist

Alright then. Death. Well, the capacity I mean is the act of death and where we go. I know you think we go to Heaven and all that and that's great. But what if you're wrong? I, personally, think death is the only definite thing in this world. And when we die, there's nothing else. There's no darkness to anyone because we aren't conscious. No dreams, no sort of 'awareness.' Our existence is finished. It's done. I think that's where the sadness of the act comes in. Because we can have all these amazing experiences in life, but death is just blackness; bleakness. Nothingness. A finish. The absolute of nothing.

Preacher

I like that phrase, 'the absolute of nothing.' Sounds like a masterpiece. Artistically speaking, of course. Sorry... You were saying?

Artist

It does. I'll have to remember that down the road. But I was just saying that a lot of people believe there's something afterward, after all this. There's no way to know that because there's never been anyone to go all the way and come back and report.

Preacher

Not technically. You brought up Lazarus a while ago. But when Christ raised Lazarus from the dead, he didn't walk around and report on anything. I get what you're saying though. I do believe there is something after, if only because Jesus, in the Bible, tells me so. He said He was going to prepare a place for us.

Artist

What about the God-walkers? Did they report on anything?

Preacher

Not really sure. The Bible never said what exactly happened other than it did.

Artist

So then do you believe in limbo and purgatory and all that?

Preacher

Not particularly. I believe that when I die, I go directly to Jesus because He's calling me home. That's the nature of our relation-ship. Like when a father lets his child come to his house, he doesn't say 'Wait out here for a nondescript amount of time until you're fit to come in.' He says, 'Come home, my child. Welcome. You are loved!'

Artist

      Is there any other way you know that other than what the Bible says? Some out-of-body experience?

Preacher

      Nope. It all comes down to faith. How much faith and trust do I have in what is written in the Bible to believe that what it says is true.

Artist

      You have to have a certain amount of faith?

Preacher

      No, no. Just faith. Fully trusting Him.

Artist

      But what if?

Preacher

      I can't afford to think like that. I can't live in 'what-ifs' when it comes to eternity. I have to believe. When time and again the world proves the matters of His word true, my doubts dissipate. They disappear because Christ *appears*. Not literally; spiritually, mentally, emotionally... all the way down to my core. Even with the chaos of late, I know beyond the shadow of a doubt that He is true, He is. He exists and He's alive!

Artist

I understand why you would want to think like that. I do. I wish I could believe in a big golden city in a far off space with angels and white horses and a big dude welcoming everyone and their mother through huge gates. I admit, there's an appeal. And it's not that I don't believe in God. I believe Jesus was real. There's just too much that backs that up. But Him being God's Son and living like God and Man at the same time and the dying and rising... all of that. There's just no way. There's nothing that backs those claims up except one book. History would say so if it were true.

Preacher

I see why you would not want to die now. Did your girlfriend think like this?

Artist

I'm not sure. It wasn't something we spent a lot of time talking about. I know she had beliefs, but they weren't defining for her. She lived life very openly. Very free-spirited. Very open with her mind and body. We both lived like that.

The Artist's voice cracks. He pauses and wipes his eyes. A moment passes and he clears his throat.

Artist

No point in having reservations if your future ends in blackness. Most of our friends were like that too. I'm the only one left of our core group though.

Preacher

Where are they now?

Artist

Well, see, that's what happens when you are the leader and everyone just wants to end it. Some committed suicide, others starved themselves, and then some... they begged for me to finish them off. How can you say no to someone you care so deeply for, that is suffering so much? I wanted them to live, but there's no cure for a bite. No cure for the infection. There was just death and darkness in their future. Nonexistence is better than the pain they were going through.

Bitten

I can relate... I still don't want that blackness though... that's... that's not better than this... at least I'm still more... or less... alive... The Preacher's future... if it's true... sounds a lot better than... what we have going for us...

Artist

It does. I can't commit to something I'm not sure of though. That's not the way I'm wired.

Preacher

What *are* you sure of?

Artist

That I'm going to die.

Preacher

Are you absolutely *sure* of that?

Artist

What kind of question is that?

Preacher

A difficult one because if you're not sure, and you say yes... then you are wired much differently than you think. If you say no, then you're being honest and still wired much differently than you think. Much of your reasoning goes in circles and constantly contradicts itself.

Artist

Heads you win, tails I lose. Something like that?

Preacher

Except this has nothing to do with a game. It's your life and your death and has nothing to do with me. I just asked a question.

Artist

What's your answer to the same

question then?

Preacher

I'm not sure I'm going to die, but...

Artist

But you're sure that if you do, then you know where you're going. Got it. What if you don't die?

Preacher

The only way that will happen is if God comes first.

Artist

And if you die, what if you come back to life?

Preacher

Then I'll probably try to bite you.

Bitten begins to laugh and cough. He holds his hand to his mouth, trying to stifle it while blood runs through his fingers. He pulls his hand away from his mouth only to sway, while the Artist and Preacher both jump up to keep him from falling out of his chair.

Part II

Artist

Is he gone?

Preacher

Almost. His heartbeat is barely there.

Artist

Is he conscious?

Preacher

No. But he's far from dead.

Artist

Well, we have to deal with him now;
before he goes, before he turns.

Preacher

We aren't preemptively striking on this.
He could have a second wind and be good for
another while.

Artist

You know that's not how this works! He's already asked us to end it for him...!

Preacher

Do we really have to go over this again? We *don't kill* the *living. Do you understand*?

The Preacher takes a defensive step toward the Artist, standing between him and Bitten, who's now closed up in the bathroom.

Artist

Easy, Deputy. You don't have to be threatening about it. We'll do it your way and then I'll say I told you so. It's not like it'll be hard to tell if he turned or not.

Preacher

Exactly. So there's no need to hurry. Let's continue our conversation. Like he was saying, it's been a nice distraction from the current situation. Where were we?

They both sit back down at their table, the weight of the inevitable on their shoulders.

Artist

You were getting ready to tell me about your thoughts on the act of death and what's after. Not like there's going to be any surprises from you. I will say that while I was resting, after we took care of Bitey, I thought of some more questions and things that might stump your reasoning.

Preacher

He's not 'Bitey' yet.

Artist

Whatever. He will be.

Preacher

Anyway. There may be some questions I don't have the answer to. Let's just start where we left off, like you said: death. 'The After.' They aren't easy subjects.

Artist

They *are* easy for a God that apparently created both though.

Preacher

Did He create death or was that a byproduct of Adam and Eve disobeying?

Artist

Hey! I said *I* had the hard questions. No 'chicken or the egg' stuff.

Preacher

Fine, fine. If we get through this, maybe one day we'll have that discussion. What you said earlier sums it up for me; if I die, I know where I'm going. I believe that in an instant I'll be called home and standing before God. Death is finite, but life ironically can be infinite. It all depends on the choices you make down here.

Artist

So you're saying that if I do good to my neighbor, I'll be alright?

Preacher

That's a way to live your life, but it's not enough. In the 'act of death' it all comes down to the decision you made in your heart about your relationship with Christ. In His death, He *gave* life. I chose to have faith in Him and let Him *have* my life. I accepted Him as my personal Savior and asked for forgiveness for my sin. He gave it to me and He gave me life. It was just a simple decision, not complicated at all. Faith, trust and belief. It's what it all boils down to. So the 'act of death' isn't really death for me. It's life.

Artist

It all boils down to being sure though. You have no concrete proof that will happen and that God really did give eternal life to you and that this 'supreme being' really exists.

Preacher

Why do you keep talking about proof? All we can do is trust that what God said in

His word is true and He really does have the whole world in His hands.

Artist

I need to *know* He exists. I *need* that proof. If God wants me, He can come and get me.

Preacher

Don't tempt Him. He may prove Himself sooner than you think. And then you're up the creek when all you had to do was stop wasting time and just let go of whatever is holding you back.

Artist

What about now though? If that's really all true, if He's *really* there, then shouldn't we be at peace and not have the creepy stalkers outside ready to bite into our skulls?

Preacher

Not necessarily. Having His hand on everything means one thing, but us giving all our fears and fates to Him is another. How we react in situations, be it continued life in front of this enemy or death because of it, defines our relationship with God. You can have peace about the 'stalkers' but that doesn't mean God will keep them from infecting you. All things work together for the good, to all those that love the Lord. My death or my life is always part of a bigger plan and I accept that. No, I don't want to be eaten. No, I don't want to be chased like a running dog. But if you ask me if I'd die to carry on God's plan, then the answer is yes. I would die if it brought you to Him somehow. That's how serious this all is. This is more serious than what ever kind of tragedy has defaced the planet.

Artist

This is pretty heavy stuff. Stuff I still don't accept, but I can see how it would make sense to a lot of people without a purpose. It still kind of sounds like a cult though. Which reminds me: what were you whispering about with what's-his-name over there in the bathroom earlier? Were you converting him?

Preacher

I don't convert. I can only share what I believe and hope and pray someone else makes the same decision. It's not begging and pleading. It has to be about the individual making their own decision in their heart to follow what they have come to believe is the truth. I can only present the facts; God has to open the heart.

Artist

So you *were* converting him!

Preacher

He made a decision. If you want to call it conversion, go right ahead. But you know it's deeper than just changing religions. You *have* to.

Artist

But even with this decision, he suffers. It sounds like you would all go through the same stuff 'non-believers' would, you just have a remedy for it. Like a common cold with a cure.

Preacher

Kind of. Except there's not a cure for it. Just like there's not a cure for that guy's infection. It will be the end of him and he will die with it. God gave us eternal life, but not an end to suffering on Earth. Things run smoother if you let Him work things, but it doesn't mean they'll be any easier.

Artist

You have *all* the answers, don't you?

Preacher

Shh. Hold on. There's some movement in the bathroom...

The bathroom door creaks and opens, with Bitten barely holding himself up against the frame.

Bitten

Fellas...

Preacher

Is it time?

Bitten

Yes...

Artist

When do you want us to take you out?

Preacher

What the crap?! That's *not* important right now.

Bitten

It's fine, Preacher... I'm at peace now... Let him do what he feels... he needs to do...

Artist

Done! He said it and it's time.

Preacher

We've already been over this! Really! Just let him be. Killing him is only going to speed up the process.

Bitten

It's OK... Really...

Preacher

I can't.

Artist

I'm going to anyway, Preacher!

Preacher

He's not even asking any more! He's putting up no fight and not pleading either way!

Artist

The only way I'm not, at this point, is if *you* kill *me*! Goodness knows, you won't. And I'm not going to stand here and wait for him to turn!

Preacher

Stand down!

Artist

The only way to do it is by removing the head or...

The Artist walks towards the bathroom where Bitten is still leaning against the frame. Bitten stands motionless, watching. Waiting.

Artist

...destroying the brain. Here. We. Go!

The Artist rears his bat, only to find the Preacher jump between he and Bitten once again.

Artist

Stop doing that! Move!

Preacher

No! No! No! Why are you so willing to do this? What are you afraid of?!

Artist

Preacher. I don't have the faith and eternal life and holy goals you do. This is what we're here to do now. Get out of my way! For the last time!

They hear Bitten slide down the frame, hitting the ground like a bag of seed. The Preacher grabs hold of the cricket bat above the Artist's head.

Preacher

Wait! Look. He's gone...

Artist

Let go of the bat!

Preacher

Will you. Sit. Down!

The Preacher shoves the Artist roughly to the ground, standing above him waiting for the Artist's next move.

Artist

Shoving like that is considered violence, Preacher!

Preacher

Violence isn't a sin.

Artist

But maybe it was in God's cards for me to kill him!

Preacher

He was going to die whether you did it or not.

The Preacher turns around to see Bitten slumped in the doorway of the bathroom, not moving. No sign of life, Bitten's arms and legs twisted and held down by his torso.

Artist

Fine! You're right!

The Artist gets up, not even bothering to brush off his pants from the dirty floor.

Artist

Now a zombie is going to come back and I could've prevented that! You could've too!

Preacher

Don't say that.

Artist

Well it is.

Preacher

I don't mean that. I mean the... 'Zed'
word. Don't say it. Call them something else.

Artist

Whatever. Just calling it like I see it.

*The Preacher suddenly jumps in the
Artist's face, nose-to-nose.*

Preacher

Will you please *stop* calling things the
way you think they are?! They don't have to
be this way or that way and certainly not *your*
way!

Artist

And they don't have to be yours! For
crying out loud! Not everyone is going to fall
for your preaching and God stuff like *he* did!
And it's about time you figured that out!

*They are standing toe-to-toe, neither
man willing to back down.*

Preacher

You're right! Fine! You think I haven't
thought about that? That's the freaking hard
part of being who I am and who God called me
to be!

Artist

Well, I'm glad you just have your *whole*

life and purpose all *figured* out! We don't all have a divine calling that makes us better than everyone else!

The Preacher suddenly realizes his temper and steps back. His shoulders lose their tension. His head hangs slightly, letting hair fall in front of his eyes.

Preacher
I was just saying.

Artist
That's all you've done is '*just say*!' You haven't convinced me of *anything*!

Preacher
I wasn't trying to convince you. I was just answering questions for you. I figured you needed those answers. I figured you wanted something.

Artist
From you?!

The Preacher shakes his head, running his fingers through his sweaty hair.

Preacher
No. From God...

Artist
You aren't getting the point apparently.

You have to believe in something in order to get something out of it. Obviously, Mr. Slumpster in the bathroom over there got something out of you. And you said he made a decision, but you never answered my question: what were you *whispering* to him?

Preacher

He asked me if I could give him what he needed to meet God.

Artist

What did you give him?

The Artist finally relaxes his shoulders and unclenches his fists.

Preacher

Nothing. He is already going to meet Him. We all are.

Artist

In one way or another, I guess we'll all meet our ends.

Preacher

On good terms or bad, yes.

Artist

And what terms is he going to meet The Big Guy?

Preacher

Based on the decision he made while we were sitting in the corner there, pretty good terms.

Artist

He converted. I was right.

Preacher

No, for the last time... A relationship with God isn't a religion or conversion. It's a conscious choice only a living soul can make.

The Artist gives a quizzically curious look, but shakes his head as if to remove the question from his mind.

Artist

Well normal people call it a conversion. Normal, non-Christian, unhappy-future people call it *conversion*.

Preacher

Then he is converted by his own belief that God is saving grace and that his eternity is sealed and he can't be taken away from God's love.

Artist

I guess he didn't like my so-called 'pessimistic' outlook then?

Preacher

You're not pessimistic. You're lonely. Every lonely person walking this earth has doubts with faults and troubled thinking. Even I do. No one is safe from that.

Artist

Nothing is safe these days then. Outside, inside; internal, external. Dangers staggering everywhere you look. Even in here... So what are we going to do about him? You wouldn't let me kill him and now he's dead. Can I kill it *now*?

Preacher

It's not an 'it.'

Artist

It's not a person either, man. It's *got* to be dealt with.

Preacher

I don't care what you do as long as his heart has stopped.

Artist

I don't think that's in question.

Preacher

I know. He's not here anymore anyway. Dead and cold.

Artist

Don't sugarcoat it or anything.

Preacher

Just let him be for a while. We're fine. It's not like *one* of them is going to be a problem.

Artist

One in here, a thousand outside...

Preacher

At least we can figure our odds. But the end is still pretty unclear. Who knows how we'll get out of this?

Artist

God.

Preacher

Well.. right.

Artist

I don't even believe it and *I* knew that.

Preacher

Think you're pretty witty, don't you?

Artist

I have my moments.

Preacher

Well thanks for stating the obvious. We still don't know how many are out there though.

Artist

It's black and white and blood red: that we do know. So, in your 'divine' opinion, what's the point of all this? What's the purpose?

Preacher

I think the better question now is: what is *our* purpose?

Artist

The question to my answer first. Why is God letting this happen?

Preacher

Beats me. I stopped trying to figure God's intentions a long time ago. What I do know is that out of every bad situation, He is always working something out for His will.

Artist

Glad He's got to kill a few billion people to further His purposes and prove a point.

Preacher

I can't say I understand Him all the time. But I know that if our friend slumped over here really meant what he said, this situation we've found ourselves in was worth it.

Artist

Really? Was it worth your family too? Just to save his behind from the frying pan?

Preacher

As much as it hurts, yes. My family is fantastic now. They are in no pain. They aren't sick anymore. They are beautiful in unimaginable ways. What God is providing for my family and this bartender is something much more than this great, green earth could ever give them. Much more than you and I could ever give. So, yes. It was worth my family. It was worth his behind.

Artist

That's a little controversial. And yet, if I believed what you believe, I think that would give me some peace. I can see a little of what's keeping you together down here.

Preacher

But goodness gracious is it hard.

Artist

I can imagine. Preacher. I'm sorry for your losses.

Preacher

And I'm sorry for yours.

Both men smile, gratefully, looking into each others eyes.

Preacher

Now to my question. What is our purpose?

Artist

The way I figure it, what it was and what it is now are two very different things. I assume it's the same for you?

Preacher

It's funny, because as a Christian, I only ever have one purpose and that is to do what God asks of me.

Artist

And what's that, specifically?

Preacher

'Go ye into all the world and preach the gospel.'

Artist

More 'Christian' words. How am I supposed to know what that means?

Preacher

Sorry. It's a habit. What that really means is that we are supposed to share with the world what God has said in His word and what it means for our eternities. It's more of a command than a purpose though. I slip up on it, I disobey it and I even run from it sometimes. Like blood, law and the undead.

But it's still what I'm supposed to do, whether I do it or not.

Artist

That's the great thing about being, what I like to call, an 'open minded-free thinker.' I get to determine my own purpose in life and I don't have to worry about dis-obeying anyone. I just have to make sure my heart's in it and one day, it'll pay off. My life can be a masterpiece or a rough draft. It can also be a huge burden. But it's mine and mine alone.

Preacher

What is it now?

Artist

I like to think it's a work-in-progress coming along nicely, but not even close to being done.

Preacher

Before all this though. Before the world changed and surviving became your life, what did you think you were meant to do?

Artist

I know I was meant to be world-renown. I was headed on the right track. The right schools, a great amount of people following my work; the right talent, the right mindset. It all fell into place and I was heading in the right direction.

Preacher

Everything was just right, huh?

Artist

Everything! I had shows in Paris, Prague, Moscow, Oslo, Warsaw and too many places to name in the U.S.

Preacher

So you *were* world-renown then?

Artist

Not like I was meant to be. My work was becoming way too commercialized and I wanted to be free of those constraints and have people just appreciate my work for what it was.

Preacher

And what was it?

Artist

Free. Open. Relatable on a grand scale! It's not always free *or* relatable when you charge admission to shows and galleries.

Preacher

I agree. What was your specialty?

Artist

I was an artistic jack-of-all-trades. I dabbled in mixed media, painting, photography... really everything. I mixed it all into fantastic mythologies and metaphors. It was a compulsion met and it was a challenge and... and people knew me!

Preacher

I'd say you had exactly what you wanted. Fame and freedom to do exactly what you felt you were meant to do.

Artist

Was it too much to ask for more though? I wanted DaVinci's legacy while I was still alive. Michelangelo's glory before I turned thirty-five. I had goals... then *they* happened.

Preacher

And your renown went the way of the world?

Artist

Yeah. And now I'm sitting in a crappily lit room with a hard-boiled Preacher, an infected corpse across from me and a horde of evil dead outside. I've fallen pretty far down the ladder.

Preacher

Are you aware of what your purpose might be now? While this pandemic exists, I mean.

Artist

And you mean besides surviving?

Preacher

Yes.

Artist

It's like you said. Surviving. That's life now. The point of living is to stay alive until it's safe to live again.

Preacher

Wow.

Artist

What?

Preacher

Nothing. That's just really profound. I understand why you think that, but why can't you live now? Why can't you accomplish something? Why does it have to be just about survival; about getting to the next safe haven?

Artist

We are forced into our predicaments and some choices are already made for us. Not by God. By *them*. It's not fate, your God or Karma... We have no choices anymore despite the existence of free will, if it ever existed to begin with. Like I said earlier, not every one has a divine purpose laid out so clearly as yours. Some people have to wing it and figure it out on their own.

Preacher

But it doesn't have to be that way. We can all still live for a goal; an ultimate endgame. You could still be an Artist despite all of this. You could *still* have the legacy you want.

Artist

What would be the point in that if people can't see it?

Preacher

Is art always about people seeing it? Is it always about recognition?

Artist

Why would I create for myself? I mean, sure, I could create something I alone could enjoy, but then it's all for my benefit. That's like you becoming a Christian and never sharing your faith. If you never told anyone about your beliefs and kept them for yourself, wouldn't that be pretty selfish? I've been given a gift and a talent, an ability, and I want to share it with the world. You want to preach about God to a group of people in a hot, humid wooden building with stained-glass windows.

Preacher

I'm not doing it for my recognition though.

Artist

Yeah, but I'm sure it was nice to hear that somebody was 'touched' by something you said in a sermon. Am I right?

Preacher

It was. And, if I'm honest, it was hard fighting the urge to let it go to my head.

Artist

So when Corpsy over there converted, what did you feel? Accomplished? Like you achieved something? Like God was happy with you and was recognizing your talent?

Preacher

Yes and no. I felt that God's love accomplished something yet again. I felt like I was achieving my purpose, and yes... I feel that God is proud of me. But I don't feel a boost to my ego. I feel like I have a new brother that I'll see again some day and we can talk and catch up. We can enjoy being in Heaven and part of God's family.

Artist

How do you know he was sincere though?

Preacher

That's not for me to decide. I can only trust what he said was heartfelt. It doesn't matter what I think though. God knows his heart. That's what matters.

Artist

Do *you* think he was sincere?

Preacher

I do.

Artist

With all my griping, with *all* my unbelief, would you trust that I made a sincere decision if I chose to?

Preacher

I would trust what you said, because that's all I have to go on.

Artist

I really don't see how you trust so easily.

Preacher

It's difficult and I judge more than trust, I confess.

Artist

We all do. And no offense, but Christians especially.

Preacher

I don't disagree and I won't fault you for judging some yourself. We come across elitist and legalistic and some of us truly are. I can only apologize for my part and ask your forgiveness for doing so.

Artist

I appreciate that.

Preacher

So you trust that I'm sincere?

Artist

Yeah. Sure.

Preacher

Why?

Artist

What else do I have to go on?

Preacher

Exactly! That's faith!

Artist

You tricked me into that!

Preacher

Nope. It was a simple progression. You just committed your first act of faith!

Artist

You make it sound like murder.

Preacher

Well, instead of committing murder today, you committed faith. I'd be ecstatic if I were you.

Artist

Don't get any ideas. I'm still not convinced of anything supernatural. You just helped me improve my character a little. That's all.

Bitten

grrrrll...

The Artist and the Preacher both jump from their chairs to the gargled sound of Bitten reawakening. The Preacher hangs his head and slowly puts his hat on.

Artist

'grrrrll...?' That's a new one on me.

Preacher

Me too...

The Artist looks back to the Preacher, only to find his right hand hidden beneath the brim of his black hat, obviously holding back tears and the bridge of his nose.

Artist

Preacher? Are you *crying*? *Why* are you crying?

Preacher

It's just sad after you've bonded so deeply with someone.

The Artist turns back towards Bitten to see the now discolored form trying to stand up.

Artist

Well, sad or not... he still has teeth and he's getting up. Want me to do it?

Preacher

No. I'll do it...

Artist

Well Fleshy, time for the Preacher to be the only one in his profession to *ever* actually be *sending* something to... Hey! What are you...?!

The Preacher has the Artist's bat in his hands while walking swiftly across the room, slowly rearing until he comes to the corpse of Bitten now almost fully upright. With a swing, Bitten falls. The Preacher swings at Bitten's head again and again and again.

Artist

Preacher, whoa... whoa...

The Preacher doesn't stop, even after the skull is caved in and brain matter is spread everywhere. The sound of wood hitting the concrete floor rings out in the room.

Artist

Preacher... !

The tall stocky figure falls to his knees and throws the bat away. He weeps.

Artist

Preacher... ?

On his knees, he suddenly takes the bottom of his fists and begins to pummel the cavity of the corpse. Still weeping, he starts mumbling and falls onto his now mutilated friend.

Artist

Enough, dude! Really! You just have to kill it! Why are you dragging it out?

The dark, bloodied figure shivers still. He gives the Artist no answer. The Artist goes over to pick up his bat.

Artist

Crap man! You messed up my bat. There's a whole *corner* gone.

Preacher

I'm sorry.

Artist

Whatever. We all have our breaking points. I was thinking you were going to beat clear through to China there for a second.

The Preacher shakily stands to his feet and looks up at the Artist.

Artist

And clean your face off, man! Gross! Angry much?

Preacher

More than I care to admit...

Artist

Apparently. But don't take it out on him. He's just fulfilling his purpose. We've all got one, remember? Oh, you stink!

Preacher

When did you become the voice of reason?

Artist

When you went all psycho. I guess the circumstances are just effecting us differently.

Preacher

Yeah...

Artist

You know what I think? Have a seat...

The Artist motions back to the table,

offering to steady the Preacher as they both find a chair.

Artist

You know what I think?

Preacher

You already said that.

Artist

Still.

Preacher

What do you think?

Artist

I think you may not want to be... but I think God would understand if you were upset with Him.

Preacher

He would understand because He's God. That doesn't make it right.

Artist

Oh, shut up. It makes you human and that's something you think He created you to be as well, right?

Preacher

Yes.

Artist

Well, Eastwood... Get angry. Say what

you need to say to Him and then be done with it. Go pray or meditate or cross yourself. Do something! You can't be running out into the masses with a chip on your shoulder. You'll die a whole lot faster like that.

Preacher

It's hard. It's so *unbelievably* hard.

Artist

But you've got purpose. You've still got to convince me, remember? You aren't done.

Preacher

I shouldn't have killed him.

Artist

You didn't kill him. That thing it became did. You killed *it*. It wasn't human or living. Get over it. Now, seriously... go over there and talk to God and get this crap sorted out.

The Preacher snorts and wipes his nose. He chuckles weakly.

Preacher

You wanna join me?

Artist

Nope. I'll take a nap or rest my eyes or something. Just try not to be snotting all over yourself and keeping me from resting. And do something about that smell! Wow!

~

Artist

Hey. Hey. Preacher... wake up.

The Preacher jolts awake.

Artist

You alright?

Preacher

Where are we?

Artist

Still inside.

Preacher

The bar?

Artist

You can't smell it?

The Preacher takes a strong whiff of his surroundings and starts coughing at the noxiousness. His eyes find the decimated body of Bitten.

Preacher

That really happened?

Artist

Uh, yeah. What was that all about?

Preacher

I'm angry.

Artist

That's been solidly established as fact around here. I'm pretty sure it has more to do with God than this world. What are you so mad about?

Preacher

I was mad about Him constantly taking people away from me. People that I love and have come to care about.

Artist

Like the headless bartender over there?

Preacher

Yeah. And my wife and little girl. We're all lonely and I guess I just let the anger take over. I'm sorry about that.

Artist

It's fine. I had to deal with it eventually too. We're only human and feelings are what make us different from all of them. Feelings are what make us different from each other. We're a kaleidoscope, you and I. Different colors that twirl in and out to make something beautiful, never fully combining, even in the midst of all this.

Preacher

You sound like an Artist now.

Artist

I like thinking positively when no one else seems to be able to.

Preacher

When did you become the optimist all of the sudden?

Artist

When I saw the optimist become a pessimist and I figure one of us had to keep our head straight. I now hand the reigns back to you.

Preacher

I don't want them.

Artist

Too bad. Optimism is exhausting. And speaking of 'back to you,' we've hinted at it and what you think you should do with your life. We just haven't discussed where you think Jesus wants *you*. Why are you a Preacher?

Preacher

That's a good question. One I ask myself every single day now. I wonder if it even matters anymore.

Artist

Someone once insinuated to me that purpose always matters.

Preacher

But the purpose of a Preacher is to minister to people and preach and lead. That's the idea at least.

Artist

So you need a fairly good amount of people for this?

Preacher

Ideally.

Artist

So if it was Sunday and I'm the only one that walked in to your church, would you still preach or would you just pack up and say that there's no point in us being there?

Preacher

I'd really feel there was no point.

Artist

That's where we are a lot alike. We want so bad for our talents and message to reach crowds, we forget about that one person that might really benefit from it.

Preacher

And here I was thinking that you needed to learn something.

Artist

Well, if I was the only one to walk into your church on Sunday and you just went home, I'd really feel that God didn't want to give me anything. Like I'm just one person and one person doesn't matter. It's all for the greater good, not for the individual.

Preacher

It's for both, but I see what you're saying. If I walked out on me, I can see how that would seem as God was walking out on me too. But the Preacher isn't God. God can use other things to bring people to Him.

Artist

What if *you* were that thing though?

Preacher

Then I'd need to be more open to it. I still have a lot to learn. About the ministry; about being human. Unfortunately, humans are fallible and selfish; we make wrong decisions. I'm supposed to be sharing His love and His teaching, but walking out would contradict that wouldn't it? I never said I *would* leave. I would consider it though, because of one factor or another.

Artist

Of course you backtrack when I call you out on it. I'm pretty sure you're not very selfish though. And you're probably the most

honest guy I've ever met. If you weren't you
and weren't open to sharing what you believe,
then that guy would have died without peace.
You, at the very least, helped give him that.
Whether I believe what you told him or not, I
have to respect it.

Preacher

If I wouldn't have argued with you, he
wouldn't have asked questions and listened to
what we had to say. I'd say God used you too.

Artist

You'd have to say He used the creepy
creepers out there too.

Preacher

'Creepy creepers?' That one's not as
good as your other ones.

Artist

Yeah, I know. What'll you do?

The Artist shrugs and smirks.

Preacher

I believe that though. I believe that all
of the circumstances leading up to our
meeting were all part of God's purpose and
that guy's purpose and even yours to some
extent...

Artist

Ladies and ghouls... the Preacher's back!

The Preacher smiles sheepishly.

Preacher

I think that's what purpose is all about. If we follow through with what we believe our purpose really is, then we don't know who it is going to effect. Be it positive or negative, it will effect and somehow infect as well.

Artist

Now I suppose that, as a Preacher, you're going to analogize the stumblers outside?

Preacher

If you already see an analogy, there's no need. Our purpose, like God, exists and is working whether we see or believe in it or not. He's there, it's there. Like them outside. Whether we see them or not, we know they are there because that's where we left them. We don't have to see a purpose to see it's effect. We didn't have to see him get bitten to know where the gashed teeth marks came from. We don't have to see God to know He loves us and is leading us in some way or another.

Artist

Kind of like fate. Fate is predetermined by some outside force and whether I like control or not, there's a lot I can't control. And fate is something I *definitely* can't control.

Preacher

But if you knew your fate, would you change it?

Artist

It all depends on my fate and whether I liked it.

Preacher

What if your fate was worse than death?

Artist

Like Hell, for instance? Like burning in Hell?

Crossing his arms, the Artist slowly leans back against the wall.

Preacher

Yes. Would you like that?

Artist

Of course not! But you can't prove to me that is going to happen. You just can't prove it.

Preacher

What are you holding on to?

Artist

Nothing. I just don't believe it. You've still offered no proof.

Preacher

I can tell you something that *is* proven. You know from all the reports, you're already infected with the virus, whether bitten or not.

Artist

There's still some debate about already being infected...

Preacher

That's not the point. Inevitably, unless they find a cure, when you die you'll turn. Being bitten just starts the process and dying just solidifies the reaction. If you never saw any of those things occur, would you believe that they were true?

Artist

I see the effects, so it would make sense.

Preacher

Seeing your eternity would make sense, but by then it would be too late to change it. I don't want it to be too late some day.

Artist

I'll take my chances.

Preacher

You're a smart guy. I can tell. Do you really want to go down that road?

Artist

There can't honestly be any worse roads to go down than the ones I've already run. If I want to see Hell, I see it out there and lying decapitated in front of me. That's the Hell I believe in and Heaven is gone. I had Heaven in my girl and in my life and where I was headed. Now it's all a burning lake and we're there together.

Preacher

Then there's nothing left for me to say. I've told you all I know and all you need to know. Whatever decision you make is up to you.

Artist

Can we stick together while we're out there though?

Preacher

Yes. We can. But there's a chance one of us may not make it much further than that door.

Artist

Speaking of, there's a light coming through the crack. It's morning. We have to go.

The Preacher looks into the Artists eyes, longing to see change.

Artist

Don't look at me like that. I've made my decision. It may change, but not right now. There's more pressing things to think about.

Preacher

I'll go as far as I can with you. If there's too many though, I don't have any gas. I'm dead in the water.

Artist

It's OK. I can swing for both of us and your blade will still take care of a couple, chain spinning or not. I have something to confess though, Preacher.

Preacher

You don't have to. I'm not a Priest. This isn't a confessional. Just share your heart. We're friends.

Artist

Thanks. I, uh... I lied.

Preacher

About what?

Artist

About the dead guy's name. I know what the sign says.

The Preacher's eyes widen.

Preacher

What does it say? What's his name?

The Artist smiles a little, then frowns and stifles his tears.

Artist

It says 'Willy's.' His name was Willy.

Acknowledgments

My Heavenly Father
Kendall Doub
H.V. Nelson
Gary Chapman
Nancy Daniel

Amy Nelson
Ressie Nelson
Van Nelson
Betty C. Nelson
Beth Nelson
Steve Parks
Deb Rock
Caleb Duvick

Ravi Zacharias
Cormac McCarthy

Author's Note

I'll acknowledge that zombies don't exist when the world acknowledges it's need for a Savior. Only one of those things can be true.

Notes

26614665R00079

Made in the USA
Charleston, SC
13 February 2014